A DAY WITH UNCLE BEMBE

By Kimberly Gordon

Copyright © 2018 by Kimberly Gordon
Illustration copyright © 2018 by Kimberly Gordon

All rights reserved. No part of this publication may be reproduced, distributed, or transmitted in any form or by any means, including photocopying, recording, or other electronic or mechanical methods, without the prior written permission of the publisher, except in the case of brief quotations embodied in critical reviews and certain other noncommercial uses permitted by copyright law. For permission requests, write to the publisher, addressed "Attention: Permissions Coordinator," at contact@5dmedia.org, or mail to:

5D Media Publishing
PO Box 10586
Westbury, NY 11590

Ordering Information:
Quantity sales. Special discounts are available on quantity purchases by corporations, associations, and others. For details, contact the publisher at the address above.

Orders by U.S. trade bookstores and wholesalers. Please contact Big Distribution: 5dmedia.org or email support@5dmedia.org.

Printed in the United States of America
A Day with Uncle Bembe / Kimberly Gordon
ISBN-13: 978-0-9989217-7-8

First Edition

Dedicated to all the little Jevaun's searching for their passion; and to all the conscious mentors who teach others even before they are ready to listen.

A DAY WITH UNCLE BEMBE

Not Your Typical Saturday Morning — 7

Off to an Interesting Start — 13

Time for Work — 19

A Whole New World — 25

Harvest Farmers Market — 31

Food Art — 43

Big Hat, Don't Care — 55

Proud — 63

The Long Way Home — 67

A Creation of my Own — 69

Chapter 1
Not Your Typical Saturday Morning

"Good Morning Jevaun," said Mr. Jones as he opened curtains to let sunlight into the bedroom. It was time for his son to begin the day. "Wake up," he continued.

"But dad, it is so early and there is no school today," Jevaun replied as he covered his head with a pillow, shielding his eyes from the sun beams now present in his room.

Jevaun wanted to wake up late, eat his favorite cereal, and play video games like he did every Saturday. But his parents had other plans for him.

"What time is it?" he whined.

"It is 6 a.m. and you have one hour to get ready."

"But it's Saturday, Dad. Ten-year-old's get to sleep in on Saturdays!"

"Saturday is just another day Jevaun.

Your Uncle Bembe is on his way to pick you up."

"Uncle Bembe?" Jevaun shouted as he rolled out of bed to find his mother. He was sure she would let him stay home.

"Mom! Mom!" He screamed as he ran around the house looking for her.

"In the kitchen," she replied. Jevaun ran down the stairs and straight to the kitchen to discuss this important matter face to face.

"Mom, do I have to go with Uncle Bembe today? He always smells funny," he said as he stomped his foot and squeezed his eye brows.

"And it's so hot outside. And my brain is still asleep," he continued.

"Yes, you do," she said. "Get dressed! Working with him will be fun."

Dad chuckled has he sat down to eat his breakfast. "Listen to your mother," he added.

"So, why are you not teaching today?" Jevaun mumbled, worried what his mother would say if she heard his questioning.

"Excuse me?"

"I mean, why does Uncle Bembe work so early; and why on the weekends?"

"Not everyone works Monday through Friday like your father and I," said Mrs. Jones. "It's only one day. Now go get dressed!"

"But I have a project to do, and I still don't know what to make it about."

Jevaun was assigned the homework a month prior and still needed to choose a topic. Now he only had 3 days left to create a project about something he enjoyed doing. And that was a challenge for him.

"You have all day tomorrow to do your project, maybe you will get some ideas today."

Knowing he would not win this battle, Jevaun proceeded as he was told.

Chapter 2
Off to an Interesting Start

Approaching each step with extreme caution, Jevaun sauntered up the stairs.

"Jevaun, are you still on the stairs?" Mrs. Jones asked 10 minutes later.

"I have to be careful mom. My legs are still asleep!" he called down to her as he turned his head to read the expression on her face.

Her eyes told him she was serious. "Okay, okay," he said has he quickened his movement up the stairs, into his room, and right back into bed.

"I know what is in each drawer, so no point in opening each one of them," he thought. From his bed, Jevaun looked around the room for a few minutes.

"Maybe I can stay home because I have nothing to wear," he said.

"Jevaun, now you only have 30 minutes. I hope you are getting dressed!" said Mrs. Jones as she made her way up the stairs to check on him.

"No Mom, I have to brush my teeth." Jevaun sprang to his feet and dashed to the bathroom to grab his toothbrush.

Mrs. Jones knew her son very well, so understood what she had to do.

"Jevaun, I know what you're trying to do. And it's not gonna work today," said Mrs. Jones as she made her way upstairs and leaned against the bathroom door.

She watched as Jevaun brushed one tooth at a time, because he felt it was too early to rush. "Why is she spying on me?" he thought to himself.

By her crossed arms, Jevaun knew his mother would not fall for any more of his tricks. As soon as he was done with the last tooth, she said, "Okay, now get dressed."

"But I have nothing to wear," Jevaun replied.

"I knew you would say that. Here, put this on," she said as she handed an outfit to him she had already picked out as back up. "You have 20 minutes, so please do not take too long."

Jevaun was dressed in less than 5 minutes but was not happy about it.

"They will not let me leave before breakfast," he thought.

Instead of informing his parents, he closed his bedroom door, hoping if he was really really quiet his parents would forget he was still home, and he could go back to sleep.

As soon as he had a complete mission planned out, the front door bell rang. It was Bembe.

"Jevaun, it's 7 o'clock. Your uncle is here. It's time to go," said Mr. Jones.

But I'm not ready yet!" Jevaun said. "I can't find my sneakers, and I have looked for them everywhere," he continued, knowing exactly where they were hidden. He was hoping his parents would understand the importance of his sneakers and allow him to stay home and play with his tablet or take a long nap.

"I found them!" Dad said, "Come down and put them on."

"But I didn't have breakfast yet," said Jevaun as he tied his shoes.

"You are spending the day on a food truck. I'm sure you will find something to eat."

Chapter 3
Time for Work

"Bye Jevaun, have fun," Mr. and Mrs. Jones said in unison, as their son walked out the door.

"You have gotten so big Jevaun," Uncle Bembe said.

Jevaun had not seen his uncle in a very long time, and he was a little happy to see him. He remembers when Bembe was a banker and wore suits every day until he quit his job and disappeared. No one understood why.

He was still tall, but now had dreadlocks that had grown at lease a foot since his last visit.

Bembe placed his hand on Jevaun's shoulder as he tossed a large burlap sack over his.

"I'll take good care of him," Bembe said as the door closed.

Jevaun noticed the twins Tommy and Raheem standing outside their house across the street, both in baseball uniforms.

"Mom, let's go!" Raheem shouted.

Jevaun remembered the last time he woke up this early on a Saturday was for an away baseball game. "They will be standing there forever. Mrs. Green is always late," he thought.

He played on the team for 5 years with them but quit after the first game this season without telling any of his friends. The twins are the last people he wanted to see.

"Did you have to show up exactly at 7?" he questioned Bembe, frustrated by his predicament. For a moment Jevaun attempted to hide behind his uncle, hoping the boys would hurry up and leave.

"Of course, I showed up on time. It's a sign to show you that you are important to me," Bembe said.

Worried his friends would see him with his "crazy uncle", and tell the entire baseball team, Jevaun continued with his questioning. "Where's your car?"

"It's a beautiful spring day," Bembe said as he waved and smiled to the boys he noticed staring at them. "We are walking today."

"Hey Jevaun, where you been?" Tommy yelled at them.

"Okay, let's go," Jevaun said as he tugged on Bembe, while acting like he didn't hear his friend. "So, what's the bag for?"

"You'll see. Just trust me," Bembe chuckled. "I hope you got your rest. I'm gonna put you to work today!"

"Work? But I'm a kid," Jevaun replied.

Chapter 4
A Whole New World

The pair made their way down the sidewalk towards the center of town. Jevaun kept checking over his shoulder making sure his neighbors had stopped staring.

Bembe looked down at Jevaun and said, "Can I ask you something? Why are you so worried about those boys back there?"

Surprised his uncle knew he was embarrassed, Jevaun responded, "What? Why would you say that?"

"I know you boy, because I was you. What do you like to do?"

"Sleep," Jevaun responded without hesitation.

"Well, you can't sleep through life. What kind of life is that? What do you love doing when you are awake?"

"Um...hum." Jevaun was not used to these types of questions. Grownups usually told him what to do, not ask what he wanted to do.

"If you don't know, you need to try new things to understand what is important to you. If you do, then you need to spend more time becoming a master of what you love. Don't worry about those guys; they just do the same thing every day. They play with that bat and that ball every day because someone told them to, and don't know no betta."

"I guess I like to paint," Jevaun mumbled.

Before moving, Bembe lived in the area for 30 years, so he knew all the short cuts to downtown.

They went behind the fire department, through a broken fence, and down the alleyway between the shoe store and ice cream shop.

"I've been down here a million times but never this way," Jevaun said, in amazement.

"There are endless ways to get wherever you want to go. This is just one option," Bembe replied.

The downtown area was usually crowded when Jevaun came with his family. With long lines of cars at traffic lights, and walkers bumping into each other on the sidewalks. But at 7:30am, it was like a totally different place. None of the stores were open.

"So, what are we doing here?" Jevaun questioned as they approached the big bank that always gave out the best lollipops. As soon as they made a sharp right into The Plaza Square, Jevaun was shocked to see so many people up that early in the morning.

"We're just in time. This, Jevaun, is where the magic begins."

They turn into the plaza, and Jevaun sees a few dozen booths set up.

"This is Harvest Farmers Market. Open at 7:30am every Saturday through the summer. I like to be the first one here. This is the largest one in your area. Farmers and business owners come from all over to bring you the best stuff. I've learned to find the Farm or Farmers

Market where ever I go. And today we're so lucky it's right here."

Jevaun was still confused but decided to just listen for a change.

"Do you know where your food comes from?" Bembe asked. "I do. If I don't, I don't make it. And if I don't make it, I don't eat it."

Chapter 5
Harvest Farmers Market

Uncle Bembe and Jevaun walked under the large white and red "Harvest Farmers Market" sign that hung from the street lights. They were the first people there that were not standing behind a table or booth.

"Heya Mr. JoJo," Bembe shouted as he waved to the little man in his 80s that sat behind the wooden booth closest to them.

"This is my nephew," he continued. "He's a bit lost."

"I'm not lost. I know where we are. It's just so early and hot," Jevaun said as he stood behind his uncle, still confused as to why they were there.

"Ha ha," Mr. JoJo chuckled as he slowly stood to his feet.

"It's alright. I was lost at your age too. Until my grandfather showed me around the farm, and I fell in love with it."

"Sounds dirty," Jevaun said as he bit off a broken fingernail and spit it out on the ground behind him.

"Dirt is natural. It is cleaner than what you are eating under your fingernails. Bembe, feed this boy!" Mr. JoJo said with a smile.

"Ewe, gross," Jevaun said when he realized what he was doing, and continued spitting, attempting to clean his mouth.

"That's exactly what I'm trying to do," Bembe said in response to Mr. JoJo.

"The usual?" Mr. JoJo asked.

"Yes sir," Bembe replied.

Jevaun watched Mr. JoJo stand to his feet to lift a blue tarp off 10 large crates in the booth. They were each filled with vegetables he recognized, but they looked funny to him. The carrots looked big – some were straight, while others were curvy and all different colors. The corn still had green leaves on them, like the ones he saw on TV, and at school in class.

Mr. JoJo gathered a bunch of fruits & vegetables - potatoes, tomatoes, spinach and a bunch Jevaun didn't recognize, and put them in bags.

"This food looks weird" said Jevaun as he watched Bembe toss the bags into his sack.

Then Bembe removed a small envelope from his pocket, handed it to Mr. JoJo, and they continued down the pathway.

The booths were all decorated differently. Some had a low music playing. A few had jewelry, while others had beads and handmade dresses.

"This is Mr. Pete. He's a baker. He makes all his breads very early in the morning, so we can have them fresh."

"Hi Mr. Pete," Jevaun said knowing that's what Bembe wanted him to do.

They pick up the usual Gluten free, wheat, rye & pumpernickel loafs, and toss it in the sack.

They continue to Christoph.

"This young man specializes in herbs, and herb seeds. Do you know why herbs are important?"

"No," Jevaun replied.

"They make your food taste even better, and they keep you healthy and strong.

We can get fresh herbs from here, but we only need the seeds."

They get Thyme, Basil, Mint, Oregano, Cilantro, Turmeric, Rosemary, Parsley and mint.

Jevaun tried to pay attention to the herb conversation but was distracted by the red and blue booth next to them.

"Uncle Bembe, can we please go over there?' He asked.

"Okay, for a few minutes," Bembe replied has he added the new seeds to his bag.

The booth was filled with comics, paintings & photographs of non-traditional superheroes. They had all types of people - young and old, boys and girls, all in super hero outfits.

"Do you know what a superhero is?" said a man wearing green framed glasses, dressed in a red and blue outfit.

"Yea. Someone with super powers who saves the day. They can fly or run fast," Jevaun answered with a smile.

"Also, someone who is good at something, and uses that power to help others. It could be anything," said the man.

"So, you're saying I could be a superhero?"

"Of course. But, first you must work hard and nurture your superpowers."

"I don't have any," Jevaun said.

"Sure, you do. You just haven't uncovered it yet. It takes time," the man said as he handed Jevaun a business card. "When you figure it out, give me a call."

"Okay, this bag is getting heavy," Bembe said when he realized the time. "It's 8:30. Time to go!"

Bembe, with his sack over his shoulder, and Jevaun with the man's business card in his pocket, left The Plaza Square in good spirts.

As soon as they turned back down Main Street, Jevaun noticed many cars were on the road.

When they made it to The Park Common, Jevaun realized a crowd was starting to form.

"What's going on today?" he asked Bembe.

"A Bob Marley Reggae cover band is playing here this afternoon. They attract my customers, so I go where they go. And today, they're here."

The two continued walking on the walking path around the large green grassy area of the common. When they reached the parking lot, they stopped. Jevaun saw nothing but food trucks and vans parked around them.

"I had to park here last night to take the best spot. People are lazy and go to the first truck they see. So, I put my healthy food right in front of the foot path, so they can think twice before ordering the garbage the other guys are selling," Bembe said proudly.

"Do you like my truck?"

Bembe's truck was a strong green color and glistened in the sunlight. "I added the yellow paint myself," he said.

Chapter 6
Food Art

Uncle Bembe tied his long hair into a bun and put on a "funny hat" before entering the truck. "And here's one for you," said Bembe as he handed a matching one to his nephew. Jevaun attempted to wear the hat as Bembe did, but it kept sliding down on all sides.

"I don't know about this hat Uncle Bembe. You have more hair than me," said Jevaun as he played with the hat.

"Figure it out," said Bembe. "Not only is it stylish, but it protects the food."

Jevaun balances the hat on his head as he follows close behind.

"So, as I was saying, I do what I love every day. I love to eat and cook. I started eating healthy and understanding food, so that's what I do for other people," Bembe said as they walked inside the truck.

The inside of the truck looks very different than Jevaun expected. He sees a garden on one side of the truck, full of vegetables and plants.

"This is my herb garden," Bembe said. "This is what I needed the seeds for - to add to my garden. See, the Cilantro and Thyme? You can never have too much Thyme."

"Now this is where my herbs and spices go. Parsley, Garlic, peppers," he said as he pointed to each one.

Jevaun didn't know what the herbs were but knew some looked like the seasonings his mom used to cook.

Bembe continued once he was sure

Jevaun was paying attention. "Here's the sink. Wash your hands."

"Over there are the Hot Plates, a freezer, a refrigerator, blender and a Juicing Machine."

Jevaun spotted upside-down pots, pans, and knives of all sizes hanging above him. And "funny looking" machines sitting on the counters.

"You're gonna spend the day with me on the truck. How does that sound?"

Jevaun didn't know what to answer, so he shrugged his shoulders. He couldn't stop thinking about the superhero booth.

"Okay, I'll take that to mean that you are excited."

"Wear those plastic gloves over there whenever you touch food," Bembe said as he pointed to a small cardboard box.

Jevaun knew he had no other options right now, besides to do what he was told.

"Wash the fruit and veggies in the sink, then put them in the ice bin," Bembe continued.

Jevaun unpacked the items from the farmers market, washed them in the sink, and placed them in their designated spots.

"Grab a piece of fruit if you get hungry, it's gonna be a long day."

"Bembe, don't you get hot in here all day?"

"Nope, never! Are you ready to learn how to cook?"

"Not Really."

"What will you do when you are a grownup if you don't know how to cook?"

"I'll go to a restaurant."

"You still need to know what to buy. How will you know which one is good to eat? You can't just go around trusting everyone."

"Okay, just show me."

"I'm just messin with you. You need to stick to the basics for today. It took me years to master my cookin. Now, its 10am. Time for me to prep the food for lunch," said Bembe. "You need to keep the fruits cold on ice always, so we have no problems. This will be your station right here. Make sure it is always neat and in order."

Jevaun's tummy was rolling with hunger now, but he didn't want to let Uncle

Bembe know. "There is nothing here I like," he thought.

"Today you are in charge of all the Fresh Juice orders. I will do smoothies, salads and sandwiches."

Bembe began chopping lettuce and fruit for the salads. Jevaun stood still for a few minutes, staring at the Juicer, overwhelmed by his newfound responsibility.

Jevaun filled the ice bin with all the fruits and vegetables. It was so colorful, Jevaun felt like he was creating an art piece.

"Just remember, clean your area. Follow the menu ingredients. Put on gloves, and juice, juice, juice."

"Okay," Jevaun said as he nodded.

"Now make me a #9 right now for practice, before we open. Remember to peel the lemons first. It's a lot easier than you think. The ingredients are right on the menu."

Jevaun dropped items into the juicer, squeezed and stirred as he was told – blending spices, fruits and vegetable according to ingredients on the menu.

"How can carrots, cayenne pepper, lemons, and all this other stuff taste good?" Jevaun asked as he emptied the mixture into a new plastic cup and inserted a straw that was conveniently placed next to his station.

"I juice because I love juicing. I only make what I love. I played around with these juice combinations for years. So everything on my menu tastes great! Go ahead, make yourself one."

"No thank you," Jevaun said, still not ready to try anything new.

"You stay hungry if you want, I'm gonna drink this one down right now," Bembe said.

Bembe drank his Fresh Juice all at once, let out one large burp, then continued to his station to slice onions, olives tomatoes, and other ingridients at his station.

Chapter 7
Big Hat, Don't Care

At 10:45am Bembe gave Jevaun two large easel boards with menu items written on them in chalk.

"Put these outside," he said.

Outside the truck Jevaun watched as Bembe opened the large order window on the side. Then Bembe tapped a button on his cell phone and Reggae music started to play from speakers on all sides.

"They're here for Reggae, so they will love my Reggae," Bembe shouted over the music.

At that moment, the truck appeared to be much larger than it did before to Jevaun. He turned toward the footpath and saw people walking their way from all directions.

"It's time. Hurry back inside boy!" Bembe instructed.

Uncle Bembe's plan was now clear to Jevaun. The ordering window was angled directly in front of the walking path. "With the music, the florescent colors, and Bembe standing so high up in the truck, they can't miss it!" he thought.

Jevaun decides to place an easel on each side of the ordering window and returns inside.

"Not all food is in season or fresh all the time, so I make changes to the menu every day. Now this is when all the hard work pays off," Bembe said.

Jevaun stood next to Bembe and watched as customers lined up for Uncle Bembe's Menu.

"Now, fix your hat so we can start taking orders."

Jevaun quickly ran to his station and stuffed his hat with paper towels.

His idea worked. The hat stood up just like Bembe's.

"Boy, you look just like me," Bembe said proudly.

At exactly 11am they started taking orders.

"Two Number 5 smoothies with Almond Milk, and a Bembe Chopped Salad Special, please," said a man wearing a bicycle helmet.

"I'll need some help on this one, just push this button right here on the blender when I say so," Bembe said to Jevaun.

"One Green Monster Juice, please," said a nice lady who wore a hat similar to the one Jevaun and Bembe were wearing.

Jevaun grabbed cucumber, a handful of Parsley, Spinach, Celery, an apple and peeled lemons, tossed them in the juicer, and pushed the button.

"Yuck, veggie juice!" he said quietly.

But, to his surprise, the lady smiled after her first sip. "Thank you," she said.

"The lady looked so happy, it can't be that bad," he mumbled to himself.

There was a small amount of the Green Monster fresh juice left over, and he was so hungry that he poured the remaining juice in a little cup for himself and took a sip.

"That's so good," he said before drinking the entire cup at once. Then Jevaun let out a big burp. Just has Bembe had done.

"Told ya," Bembe said, proud his nephew tried something new.

Chapter 8
Proud

Bembe and Jevaun served customers of all ages for the next 5 hours. When the lined started getting long, customers started dancing around the truck, and happily waited.

"There's only a few people left in line," Jevaun said around 4pm.

"It's because the show is over for the day, and we fed everyone already," Bembe teased.

"Now what?" Jevaun asked.

"We pack up and do it all over again tomorrow," said Bembe.

"Any more work for me to do Uncle?'

"See if you can take care of the last customer all by yourself," Bembe said with a wink.

It was the same lady with the hat that ordered in the morning.

"Hi, can I please have one more Green Monster juice for the road? That was the best juice I ever had!"

Jevaun was so proud of himself, and so was Bembe. He made the Fresh Juice and drank the leftovers as he had done earlier in the day.

Bembe was his mother's brother, and never had any children. He wanted to be there for his nephew and expose him to his day. This he had done.

They took off their hats and smiled for a picture for the local newspaper.

"Is it really working when you do what you love?" Bembe said as they smiled for a picture, "I call this living."

Jevaun and Bembe each enjoyed a salad and veggie sandwich on Rye bread together. They laughed and joked about all the different people they met that day. Then they cleaned the truck, returning it to its' original condition. By 5pm they were done.

Chapter 9
The Long Way Home

Uncle Bembe and Jevaun headed back down Main Street, and behind the fire department. This time they cut through a football field and watched a game for a few minutes as they passed by. They proceeded through a new alley and back to Jevaun's street.

Instead of worrying if Tommy and Raheem would see him, Jevaun started running home. He was so excited to tell his parents about his day with Uncle Bembe.

"Mom. Dad. Everyone was so friendly and happy today. I met so many people and had too much fun," Jevaun said as soon as the door opened.

"Dad, can I go back on the truck with Uncle Bembe tomorrow?"

"But tomorrow is Sunday Jevaun."

"Sunday is just another day Dad," he said.

Chapter 10
A Creation of My Own

Bembe stayed at a hotel for the evening, and Jevaun returned to his bedroom with a new purpose. He could watch his TV shows or play games on his tablet until bedtime, but chose not to. He had a long day but had no desire to sleep.

Instead Jevaun took out his art paper from under his bed and started to paint.

He was focused on creating something just like his uncle had. "Bembe loves food, and I love to paint." he thought.

"I love comics. I love superheroes. And I love to paint!" he said to himself. He had an idea.

Over the next 3 hours Jevaun created a comic book packed with superheroes. His mom and dad. Mr. Jojo and Christoph. Mr. Green Glasses. And of course, Jevaun and Bembe. He named the comic "A Day with Uncle Bembe."

When it was complete, Jevaun shouted "I love this," and ran downstairs to show his parents. He completed his school project, did what he loved, and it was still just a Saturday.

Uncle Bembe's Smoothies

Choose a Mixer:
Almond Milk, Apple Juice, Orange Juice, Pineapple Juice

Select 1 combination

#1 Double B – Beets, Strawberries & Blueberries

#2 Orange Fusion – Orange, Carrot & Mango

#3 Detox – Green Apple, Kale & Banana

#4 Caribbean Boost – Pineapple, Coconut & Orange

#5 Mango Magic – Orange, Pineapple & Mango

Uncle Bembe's Juices

#1 **Green Monster:** Spinach, cucumber, celery, parsley, apple, lemon, ginger

#2 **Forever Young:** Apple, carrot, cucumber, kale, plain almond yogurt, ice

#3 **Energy Booster:** Carrot, beets, spinach, cucumber

#4 **No Sick Days:** Orange, carrot, lemon, ginger

#5 **Ginger Time:** Cucumber, beets, apple, lemon, ginger

#6 **Mr. Clean:** Apple, beets, parsley, lemon, ginger

#7 **Aches Be Gone:** Carrot, spinach, kale, celery, beets, parsley, cucumber, garlic, ginger, cayenne

#8 **Easy Peasy:** Carrot, spinach, kale, celery, beets, parsley, cucumber, garlic, cayenne

#9 Breathe Easy: Carrot, spinach, kale, celery, garlic, radish, lemon, ginger, cayenne

#10 De: carrot, spinach, kale, beets, parsley, garlic, cucumber, cabbage, cayenne.

#11 Stress Free: Carrot, spinach, celery, beets, parsley, cucumber, garlic, cayenne

#12 Summer Time: Carrot, spinach, kale, beets, parsley, garlic, cucumber, cayenne, ginger

Fresh Squeezed Orange Juice

Fresh Squeezed Lemonade

www.ingramcontent.com/pod-product-compliance
Ingram Content Group UK Ltd.
Pitfield, Milton Keynes, MK11 3LW, UK
UKHW041448180426
11946UKWH00001B/7